His Mother's Nose

story and pictures by Peter Maloney and Felicia Zekauskas

Dial Books for Young Readers New York

THIS BOOK IS DEDICATED TO ALL THOSE WHO HAVE MADE US WHO WE ARE. AND SO, IN NO PARTICULAR ORDER AND WITH APOLOGIES TO ANYONE NOT MENTIONED, WE DEDICATE THIS BOOK WITH AFFECTION AND GRATITUDE TO Raymond Zekauskas, Jean Maloney, Felicia Zekauskas, Joseph Maloney, Jeffrey Zekauskas, Jane Maloney, Dr. Raymond Zekauskas, Mark Maloney, Tobi and Michael Sznajderman, Claudia Sandoval, Jean Molfese, George Christiansen, Miss Havey, Mrs. Ferrante, Mary Robinson, Tom Cantone, Patty Baldi, Brian DeWitt, Eddie Roth, Mark Puglisi, Rich Verderame, Lew Blaustein, Carl Gerdes, Barbara Good, Robert Curtis, ABZ, Charles Bozian, Nell and Frank Akscin, Bob Santoro, Bob Sealy, Greg Gastman, Mrs. Parker, Ed and Betty Corley, Laurie Peterson, Darlene Griggs, John and Phyllis Zekauskas, Books of Wonder, Linda and Jeanne Molfese, Ed and Margie Duffy, Betsy Rovegno, Joni Mitchell, Kitty Orsini, Dan Richards, Dave Shannon, Coaches Lippi, Lawler and Lorenzo, George Jenkins, Mike Geltrude, Maraliese Goosman, Patty and Paul Cecere, Jean Pierre Sempé, Lisa Bisk, Tom Seaver, Blanche Chernesky, Richard Corley, Susan Atran, The Cileks, David Wine, Art Rittenberg, Anne Stillwaggon, Robert Louey, Suzanne Plump, John Coleman, Alf Christiansen, Wilhemina Christophersen, David Dufford, Cliff and Garry Marine, Fran Bouchoux, Atha Tehon, Lisa Schroeder, Marco Sznajderman, Cheryl Best, Diane Petzke, Steve Leminelle, Godfrey and Dorothy Schroth, Jack Soltis, Mark Foster, Peg Brubaker, Ed Sorel, Keith Sloboda, Paul Murray, Rick Nulman, Paul Brustofski, Donna Peterman, Marius and Sue Sznajderman, Susan and Tommy Lynch, Dawn Buzash, Stasia Plump, Joya Fennell, Hugh Moore, Harriet The Spy, Wendy Alling, Mrs. Wafle, Mrs. Hoy, Wayne Gretzky, Melanie Freundlich, Terry Brandolin, Brad Tenney, Tom Two Arrows, Debra Schmitt, Woody Allen, Kimi Weart, Daria and Mindy, Dr. Doyle, Tufton Mason, Lisa Gillespie, Phyllis Fogelman, Tim Moses, Diane Arico, Gary Duschl, Dr. Seuss, Joe and Anne Cutrone, Jim Wynd, Linda Frotton, Richard Burt, Amy Peterson, Debbie Grossman, Nina Kondo, Janet Naginey, Tri-Delta, Connie Trifiletti, Mark Russo, Ernie Califano, Laurie Mullen, Michael Remus, Ian Copeland, Ray Davies, Nancy Dwyer, Deena Miller, Chris Evert, Sarah Hardie, Warren Solow, Denis Johnson, Marty Liquori, Ted Chin, Cindy Green, Maria Trice, Charlie Culp, Laura Hollomon, Nancy Wolff, Bob and Mary Brown, Antonella Cosani, Sophie Genest, Paul Spadaro, Meg Hayden, Brigitte Pincelli, Nancy Paulsen, and, of course, Bob Puddicombe • Published by Dial Books for Young Readers, A division of Penguin Putnam Inc. • 345 Hudson Street, New York, New York 10014 • Copyright © 2001 by Peter Maloney and Felicia Zekauskas, All rights reserved • Designed by Kimi Weart, Text set in Bodoni, Printed in Hong Kong on acid-free paper • 1 2 3 4 5 6 7 8 9 10 • Library of Congress Cataloging-in-Publication Data, Maloney, Peter, date. • His mother's nose / Peter Maloney and Felicia Zekauskas. p. cm. • Summary: A young boy is told that he has his mother's nose, his father's eyes, his uncle's head for numbers, and other traits from different family members, but he comes to realize that there is nobody quite like him. • ISBN 0-8037-2545-0 (hardcover) • [1. Identity—Fiction. 2. Family life—Fiction. I. Zekauskas, Felicia. II. Title. • PZ7.M29735 Hi 2001 • [E]—dc21 00-063861 • The art in this book was created in gouache, pencils, and lots of erasers.

From the day Percival Puddicombe was born, he was not his own man.

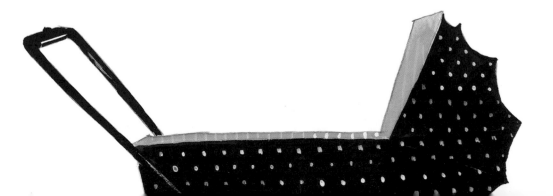

*Every*one
who saw
Percival saw
something of
themselves
in him.

"He has *my* nose!"
said his mother.

"He has *my* eyes!" gushed his father.

"He has *my* mouth!"
said his sister.

"He has *my* hair!"
cried his brother.

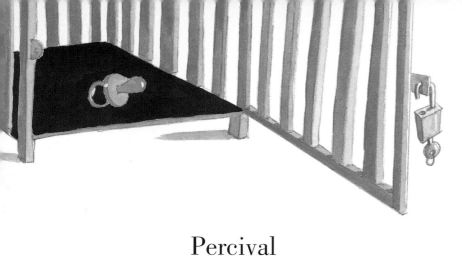

Percival
quickly outgrew
his carriage
and playpen, but
he could not escape
those who saw something
of themselves in him.

"He may have *your* nose,"
said his aunt to his mother,

"but he has *my* ear for music."

"He may have
your ear for music,"
said his uncle
to his aunt,
"but he has *my* head for numbers."

Teachers were amazed by Percival.
They'd never heard of a kindergartner who could add, subtract,
multiply, and divide—
in his head!

"Actually, it's not *my* head," Percival told them. "It's really my uncle's."

At the barber shop,
no one even
asked Percival
how he wanted
his hair cut.
The barber just cut it—
"Same as your brother's."

FOR GUISE AND GALS

STORE
HOURS
9-6

Tired
of hearing
about
everyone
else's
features,
Percival
decided
to disguise
himself.

But
his disguise fooled no one.
"Look—it's Percival!" his sister cried.
"And he's got Uncle Groucho's eyebrows . . . and moustache!"

That's it!

"I've had it!" cried Percival.
And he stormed out of the room.

"Well!" said his mother to his father.
"It looks like Percival has *your* temper."

In his room . . .
Percival looked
into the mirror.
All he could see was
his mother's nose,
his father's eyes,
his sister's mouth,
his brother's hair,
his aunt's ear for music,
and his uncle's head
for numbers.
"Where do I fit in?"
he sighed.

The next morning
the strangest thing
happened.

His mother's nose . . .

his father's eyes . . .

his sister's mouth . . .

all disappeared!

And
so did his
aunt's ear
for music . . .

and
his uncle's head
for numbers.

That evening the whole family cried about what they were missing.

Then they realized what was missing most:

Percival!

The
family looked
e v e r y w h e r e ,
but Percival was
nowhere to be found.

At the Bureau of Missing Persons, a sketch artist tried to draw a picture of Percival. But he drew a complete blank.

Meanwhile
Percival was miles away,
heading toward
the only people
who always saw him
as himself.

"Percival!"
cried his grandmother.
"Your mother just called
and said you were missing.
And so is her nose!"

"Her *nose*?"
said Percival.

"Yes—
her nose,
   your father's eyes,
   your sister's mouth,
   your brother's hair,
   your aunt's ear
   for music, and
   your uncle's head
   for numbers—
   they're all gone!"

"But *I* have them," said Percival.

"*You* have them? Where did you get that idea?"

"From them," answered Percival.

"Hmmm!" said his grandmother. "Grandpa—the family photo album, please!"

And there, on
the faces of long-lost uncles,
great-great-grandparents, and
cousins twice removed,
Percival saw *all* his family's
features, from his mother's nose
to his brother's hair.

And for the first time
Percival realized

that there was a little bit
of everyone in everybody.

When Percival arrived home, the whole family jumped for joy.

"Mom—
I've found your nose,"
he cried.
"And that's not all!"

And as Percival flipped the pages of the family photo album, an amazing thing happened:

His
mother's
nose,

his
father's
eyes,

his
sister's
mouth,

his
brother's
hair,

his
aunt's ear
for music,

and his
uncle's head
for numbers

all reappeared!

"Percival!" they cried. "You've saved the whole family!"

And as his mother hugged him, she
whispered softly in his ear:

"Percival Puddicombe,
there's nobody quite like you!"